Shadow

Shadow

GHITA EL MERNISSI

PARTRIDGE
A Penguin Random House Company

To order additional copies of this book, contact
Toll Free 800 101 2657 (Singapore)
Toll Free 1 800 81 7340 (Malaysia)
orders.singapore@partridgepublishing.com

www.partridgepublishing.com/singapore

Contents

1

Star

My name's Star. I am twelve years old, and I live in Sydney, Australia. I have always wanted a pet, preferably a cat or a dog, but my parents said that pets are a nasty, smelly nuisance. Anyway, enough about me. Let's talk about Shadow.

Shadow is the cat I found while I was running away from a forest fire.

I should probably tell you the whole story. I was going for a walk in the woods when I heard a cat yowling. The sound was coming from a tree not far away from me. I peered all around it and even climbed up the tree to see if the cat was hidden in the branches or something.

Then I realised there was a hole in the ground; it was about half a metre wide, ten centimetres deep, and filled with mud. I jumped down from the tree and looked into the hole. I saw a little black face with emerald-green eyes staring back at me. The cat meowed louder, almost as if it were trying to warn me of something. That's when I smelled smoke behind me. I swivelled around on my heel and saw a huge fire quickly advancing towards me.

I scooped up the little black cat and held it tightly in my arms. I ran out of the woods and straight to the police station, the kitten still clutched to my chest. When I arrived, I breathlessly panted, 'Fire … in woods. Found kitten … Help!'

'Whoa! Slow down, darling. Breathe in; breathe out. There we go. Now, what were you trying to tell me?' the officer asked.

'There's a fire in the woods! A big one!'

The policeman pressed his buzzer to alert the fire station about the fire.

'Now, what's your address, missy? I need it to help get you home. The streets are bad places for young children like you. I'll need your name and age too.'

'My name is Star. I'm twelve.' I then gave him my address on Salwar Road.

'Pardon? That house just burned down a couple of hours ago! Oh, I'm so sorry …' His voice trailed off. I just stood there dithering, my mouth open. Then my brain realized how serious this actually was, and the questions overflowed in my brain without pause: Was my family OK? Was the entire house gone? Where was I going to stay?

I tried to say something, but my mouth just kept opening and closing like a goldfish in shock.

The cat meowed and looked up at me with her perfect little eyes, and she pawed my T-shirt. It was almost as if she were trying to comfort me. I buried my face in her silky fur and blinked back the tears that stung my eyes. I saw the policeman's face and knew he was wondering whether to send me to a children's home or try to find someone to foster me.

'Sweetie, I'm sorry to tell you this, but your family did not survive the fire. You're going to have to go to a children's home,' he said.

In the police car ride over to the children's home, I thought over a name for the black kitten. I tried to push all negative thoughts about the fire out of my head and focused on the small cat nestled in my arms.

I decided to call her Shadow because her fur was pitch black and her emerald eyes contrasted eerily with her fur, like the moon casting a beam of light across a dark street at night.

When I arrived, I was greeted with a hug and a very warm welcome to the Sydney Children's Home. It was a large whitewashed building with a mural of a large smiling sun which I assumed was their logo. The woman told me that her name was Stevie and she would be my social worker. She was wearing a pink-and-purple leopard print shirt, which not everybody can look good in. She was also wearing light blue jeans with what looked like a ketchup stain on the left leg.

She was short but thin and had the hair of a boy, but she still managed to make it look feminine. I asked her if I could keep Shadow, and she shifted uncomfortably from one foot to the other. I realized my chances of keeping my new-found pet were slimming, so I decided to use my famous teary puppy eyes.

'Let's see her,' said Stevie, sighing. As if on cue, Shadow popped her little head out of my backpack, where I had been hiding her. I put her on the floor so she could sniff around and get used to her surroundings while Stevie oohed and ahhed.

'Aw, what a sweetheart! She's the most adorable cat I've ever seen!' She carried on like this even after Shadow jumped back into my arms and fell fast asleep, making little purring noises of appreciation. I asked Stevie if I could have some money to buy Shadow a collar, a lead, and some food. She said yes and gave me directions to the nearest grocery store. (I'd never had a cat before, but I didn't think it was fair that dogs were walked and cats weren't.)

I was worried that Shadow wouldn't want to come, but she was happy enough just sleeping in my arms for the first few minutes and then walking alongside me for the rest of the five-minute walk. At the nearest store, I asked, 'How do I get to the pet aisle?'

I bought Shadow a midnight-black leather collar with a crystal moon pendant and the name SHADOW engraved on it. I also bought a black-and-white striped lead. Then I walked in the opposite direction of the home and found an old mattress near a garbage bin.

I settled the mattress in a cosy dimly lit corner in an alleyway and laid Shadow down on it. It was small and settled into the alleyway well. I couldn't take Shadow to the supermarket with me, no matter how much I wanted to. I used to cycle to that supermarket, and there was a strict no-pets rule.

I left to buy some cat food and my dinner, hoping that I had enough left for at least a bag of crisps or a chocolate. I crossed my fingers the whole time, hoping that she wouldn't get lost or stolen. If that happened, I would officially be the worst pet owner in the world.

When I came back, I saw that Shadow had made a cat bed out of my mattress. There were about fifty cats snoozing together, with Shadow right in the middle.

'Wow,' I whispered to myself. Just then, Shadow lifted her head and smiled at me. Well, at least I *think* she smiled. I emptied the cat food out onto the ground, and all the cats immediately woke up, smelling the meat.

But Shadow pushed past them all and growled at any cat that refused to move or stood in her way. She was one of the smaller cats, but she clawed the cats that were eating some of her food determinedly. When she reached it, there was only about half the bowl left. Her collar pendant looked beautiful in the moonlight, and it jangled with each step Shadow took. *Strange,* I thought. *I was sure it didn't come with a bell.*

I don't know why, but I decided not to go back to the children's home.

After a few weeks of living on the streets, it was nearly Christmas. The roads were decorated with lights and bows. I earned money by doing dances I learnt at my old school, and Shadow just hunted for her food. Everyone was happy – except for me. The carol singers were starting to get on Shadow's last nerve, and she even attacked some of them. (Guess she hates Christmas too!) But yesterday a woman stopped and asked where my parents were. I was sitting on a bench under a tree, slurping a smoothie I got from a kiosk, and I guess she must have been suspicious. Here's how the conversation went:

'Where're your parents, young lady? Children like you shouldn't be sent out at the best of times!'

'I-I don't have any parents.'

'I beg your pardon. Do you mean you live on the streets alone?'

'Not entirely alone, ma'am. I have my cat, Shadow,' I tried to explain.

'Oh, forget about the stupid cat. It's not needed in this situation! You're coming with me right this instant!

Honestly, kids these days behave in such a ridiculous manner!'

That's when I lost it. How dare she talk smack about Shadow like that! I was so frustrated that I grabbed her purse – I needed the money for a jacket, as it was snowing lightly – stuffed Shadow into it, and ran down the road with it. The large woman shouted after me, her chubby face red, but she made no attempt to run after me.

2
Bullies

As I rounded the corner, I buried my face in my hands and cried. Shadow meowed from inside the purse. Something was wrong. Shadow had only meowed like that when she was tired or when someone was near me. I looked up, my face tear-stained and snot dripping from my nose, and was shocked. Standing in front of me, short but looming over me, was Stevie.

Great, I thought. *Just great.* I hugged my knees and bit my lip. I tried to hide in my holey sweater, but she had already seen my face. Having a black cat running around your ankles and meowing like a siren didn't lighten the mood at all.

'Just *what* are you doing sitting in a dark alleyway at eight o'clock in the morning? You've had us worried sick! These last few weeks, we've had all sorts running round looking for you! The police have been wandering round your room trying to find out where you were! They had bloodhounds, Star! Bloodhounds! Why on earth did you run away?'

'Stevie, I kinda got a little lost,' I lied.

'Well, all right then, but I doubt it,' Stevie huffed.

As we drove back to the home, I realized something: where the heck was Shadow?

'Stevie! I left Shadow in the alleyway where you found me! We need to go back *now*!' I shouted.

'What on earth? Sit down, Star! And stop that screaming!' she said.

'No! I want Shadow back! I want Shadow back *now*!' I punched Stevie's seat and kicked it hard.

'Ow! Okay, okay, I give up! We'll go back for Shadow. Happy now, Little Miss Fit?' she sighed.

We made a U-turn and parked right by the alleyway where Stevie had found me.

'This is a waste of time. She won't be here. She'll have wandered off by now,' Stevie said.

To be honest, I believed her, but to my surprise, Shadow was still sitting there. The most amazing part, though, was that she had a bunch of coins at her feet.

She was sitting there in the pose of the sphinx, and people were throwing coins at her! They must have thought she was pretending to be a statue. She looked at me with a proud look on her face, and for a second,

I could've sworn she smiled at me. I bet Stevie felt horrible now.

'What? How? But …?' Stevie stuttered as she stared out of the minivan's window.

'Yes! I told you so!' I ran out of the minivan and pulled a face at the huge smiling yellow sun on the side of the van. The logo looked horrendous, as the dodgy boys from the neighbourhood had spray-painted rude words on the faded yellow rays coming off the sun. I picked Shadow up and held her in my arms, and she fell fast asleep. But before that, I scooped up all the coins into the small pocket in the back of my backpack.

I put her in the large space in the back of the van, which was usually used to carry art or music supplies. She looked so sweet and peaceful that I could have just stood there looking at her all day long. I climbed in the back and sat there with Shadow on my lap for the whole two-hour drive back to the home. I had forgotten how far I had wandered. After all, we moved location almost every three days.

We could hear the commotion inside, and just as Stevie unlocked the gates, a football crashed straight through the window. The blue-stained glass shattered everywhere, and I leapt back, covering Shadow with my hands.

'What on earth!' Stevie shouted. Turned out that the woman Stevie asked to keep the kids entertained while she left to look for me was going crackers trying to calm the kids down.

'Good lord, what now?' huffed Stevie. I hugged Shadow to my chest and walked meekly behind Stevie, not wanting to wake Shadow. But despite my efforts, the second we stepped in, Shadow let out a loud meow because of the noise.

It was absolute pandemonium inside. Boys were jumping on the sofa and grabbing sodas from the staff fridge. A couple of guys had even started an indoor footy match! I was the only girl under fourteen in there. The other girls were probably in their room putting makeup on and doing their hair.

'Stop this madness right now!' Stevie shouted. She probably wasn't used to raising her voice, for she turned bright red in the face. For a few moments, everyone was quiet. Then Shadow let out a tiny mew. All the others stopped in their tracks, including me.

'What's that thing doing in here?' said the boy closest to me, poking and prodding Shadow.

'Leave off!' I said. 'Haven't you seen a cat before?'

'All right, Miss Hoity-Toity! You go up to your room and find a place for that cat to sleep,' said another worker. I trudged up to my room and locked the door. Then I took my sketch pad and started to draw a picture of Shadow. The sketch pad was a gift from Stevie, and I loved drawing on it.

I don't mean to sound boastful, but it turned out pretty well, if I do say so myself. I took out the coins that Shadow had somehow earned and jingled them about in my hands, deciding what to buy with them. I eventually decided to spend them on Shadow because she had earned them. I would buy her a toy.

There was a vet just down the road, but Stevie said that I would have to leave Shadow at home.

'What? Why? It's her toy I'm buying, so she should be able to come!' I said.

When Stevie and I were halfway through our argument, another girl walked through the door with Eliza, a member of the staff, behind her. The girl was young, about six or seven, and was very small, with fiery red hair and pale skin.

'Hello, Stevie. This is Rose. She's new. I was wondering if a could speak to you for a bit while Star looks after Rose, considering the fact that she isn't busy looking after that mangy cat.' She said the last bit in a cruel voice, her eyebrows raised at me.

'Sure, Eliza. Star, take Rose with you to the shops and buy her something nice,' Stevie gabbled, pressing a ten dollar note into my hand. Knowing her, she probably wanted to get as much information as she could about Rose: where she used to live, how old she was, and why she was here. After all, Eliza was the one who got all this info and passed it down to Stevie.

I introduced myself but decided not to tell her about Shadow. She might pull her tail! Anyway, we made small talk, and I found out that Rose was from the small and sweet neighbourhood two blocks down from my old house. Plus, she used to have thirteen hamsters. Thirteen! As I led Rose out the front door and down the street, she stopped in her tracks.

'Rose? Come on – stop messing about. What is it?'

'Kitty! Going into the butcher shop!' she said, pointing.

'What?' I looked and there was Shadow, trotting into the butcher shop. 'Shadow!' I shouted, running across the road, dragging Rose behind me. I reached the butcher shop and saw Mr Jo, the butcher that we used to buy our meat from when I lived in my old house, feeding Shadow a sausage.

'Mr Jo, I'm so sorry. I don't know how she got out of my room!'

'She's your cat?' said Mr Jo and Rose simultaneously.

'Kitty!' squealed Rose, and she rushed to the counter, where Shadow sat watching us curiously.

'She's a right beauty, that cat. Not a patch on my two fat kittens at home,' he said, stroking her. Shadow seemed to enjoy all this attention and purred and rubbed herself on Rose's arm, making everyone in the butcher shop smile.

I picked Shadow up in one arm and held Rose's hand with the other. We went to the twenty-four-hour corner shop down the road that housed wizard hats and giant stuffed oranges. We got lots of things. I bought a feather toy that Shadow was mesmerized by, a little Minnie Mouse comb for Rose, and a giant stuffed panther for myself. When we got back, Stevie saw that I had Shadow on top of the giant panther and went absolutely mental!

'I thought I told you to leave Shadow here, did I not? And look at the size of that toy! I can hardly imagine how much it cost! Where is my change? I said only spend five dollars!' She went on like this until Rose and I sneaked off to the kitchen to feed Shadow.

'When did you get the kitty? How old is she? What's her name?' gabbled Rose, asking endless questions the entire time we were in there. I ignored her. As I went to slink off alone into my room, I ran into Eliza, who shrieked in horror just because Shadow licked her arm. She jumped out of my arms and skittered off.

'Keep that filthy thing away from me! It's not even allowed here! It's a miracle that Stevie's letting you keep the dirty thing,' she went on. When she had finally finished her mad rant, she breathed out and straightened her back. With her grey blouse and pencil skirt, she looked more like a school librarian rather than a member of the staff at a children's home.

'Oh, and one more thing. You'll be sharing your room with Rose,' she said.

I was a little shocked at that, but I guess it was better than sharing with one of the boys. They had been teasing Rose horribly ever since we got back, saying things about her accent and calling her names like Carrot

Head, Carrot, and Marmalade just because she had red hair.

Later that night, Rose was sleeping soundly in the little bed next to mine. Shadow purred quietly on her makeshift cat bed of newspaper and the stuffing from pillows. It was then that I decided to stick up for Rose.

I'd felt angry when the boys were mean to her, but I hadn't been brave enough to face the strong beefy lads of sixteen who still ate boogies when they thought no one was looking. It had only been a couple of days, but they had called her every bad name I can think of. So the next day, when I heard the guys teasing Rose – they called her a little squirt and pushed her over – I immediately ran up to them. I must have had a strong look of fury in my eyes because half the lads ran off.

But Brodie, the leader of the gang, stood his ground. I came up to him and waited while he looked at me then laughed.

Rose was cuddling Shadow and grinning while leaning against the kitchen table happily.

'Well, hello there, Little Miss Angry Pants! You come to stick up for your little friend Carrot Head here, eh?' he laughed.

Then I did something I never would have done before I formed my bond with Shadow and Rose. I slapped him hard round the face.

'Ow!' he shouted.

He put his hand up to his face in shock, and I heard Rose gasp behind me.

'Star! How could you? And in front of Rose too!' I heard a voice say. That voice belonged to Stevie.

Uh-oh, I thought. *Busted!*

3

Trouble

A few minutes later, I found myself in Stevie's office, which was more like a day care than an office. While Stevie was lecturing me about my behaviour and saying how disappointed in me she was over and over again, I looked around her room. There was light pink wallpaper and a white fluffy rug on the ground. Her file cabinet had a big white cross-eyed teddy bear perching on top of it, with a pale brown bunny squashed between its paws. There was an old radio on her desk, as well as a framed photo of Stevie and a huge golden retriever rubbing itself on her legs. When Stevie had finished, I asked her what the dog's name was.

'Oh, that's Honey. I still have her with me at home. She's the sweetest dog you'll ever meet. Anyway, are you okay with sharing your room with Rose? Is she afraid of Shadow? We will speak about the slapping later.'

'Ha! Rose is everything but afraid of Shadow. I left her with Rose, so if you don't mind, I'll be going now.'

'Cheeky baggage,' said Stevie, but she let me go, calling to me to come back in half an hour to apologize to Brodie. Ha! Fat chance of that happening! When I got back to my room, I saw Rose sound asleep on the double bed and Shadow waiting beside the door.

'Aw, come here you cheeky devil!' I picked Shadow and played with her for an hour until she padded over to her bed and snuggled down. By that time, I was tired too, and I went to bed with Rose on one side and Shadow on the other. The next morning, I woke up because Rose was shaking me and poking me in the face while shouting in my ear.

'Star! Wake up, Star! Shadow's missing! I woke up because I needed to use the bathroom, and she wasn't in her bed! I've looked all over the home, and I still can't find her!'

I snapped to attention at that.

'What? What do you mean? Are you sure she's really gone? Oh gosh, what am I going to do?'

Rose started crying, snot dripping down her nose and tears rolling down her cheeks. I fetched a handkerchief, mopped her face, and then threw on my jeans and T-shirt and ran down the stairs

'Star, I want to look for the cute kitty, too!' she shouted after me, eager as always.

'Oh, okay, but be quiet. Stevie might hear, and it's two in the morning.'

Rose came down wearing a skirt and a top, and we set off hand in hand. I asked the very few passers-by if they had seen a black cat with green eyes and a moon collar, but they all said no. Rose suggested the park, so we found our way there and suddenly, surrounded by a very large ring of angry squirrels, I saw Shadow. There were a lot of squirrels, about seventy-five in all.

'Kitty!' screamed Rose, rushing towards her. All the squirrels turned towards her, and she backed away, hiding behind me.

'Don't make any sudden movements,' I whispered. I inched my way forward while the squirrels chattered and unsheathed their claws.

'Ah, they have pointy nails!' Rose suddenly shrieked. At that second, all the squirrels lunged for us. Then Shadow let out an ear-splitting yowl that made all the squirrels stop and run up various trees in a frenzied panic.

Rose squeezed my hand and walked towards Shadow. She immediately ran towards us and pounced onto my T-shirt, her little claws digging into the fabric. She trekked her way up until she reached my shoulder, where she perched proudly like a parrot on a pirate's shoulder. Rose squealed and patted her soft little head as we sat on a bench and caught our breath.

'I don't like those squirrels. They were mean to me. They're scary!' she said, glancing at the trees where most of the pack had run up. She suddenly gasped and pointed at a hole in the ground.

'Rose, what is it?' I asked. Shadow seemed intrigued by the little pit too, and she hopped off my shoulder and carefully made her way towards it.

'Another kitty! A white one!' said Rose.

'Really? Where?' I walked towards the pit and saw that she was right.

There was a small pure white cat in the muddy pit, but you couldn't tell because she was covered in mud. Well, we could only tell she was white *after* we washed her off. And by we, I mean my cat. Shadow was licking her clean and nudging her out of the hole.

'Ooh! Can she be my kitty? I want to keep her so bad!' Rose squealed.

'Okay.' I picked up the kitten and took her over to the water fountain for a quick rinse. When she was sparkling clean – well, *sort of* sparkling clean – I handed her to Rose and let her cuddle with the cat until we eventually made our way back to the home.

I didn't realize how long we had been gone because I didn't take my watch, but it must have been about three of four hours, judging by the fact that it was eight in the morning and Stevie was pacing the floor like a caged tiger.

'Rose! Star! Where on earth were you? We've been worried sick about you ever since you didn't come down to breakfast!' she cried. 'Wait a second … What's that you're holding, Rose?' she asked slowly.

'It's my new kitty! We found her in the park after we saved Star's kitty and got attacked by mean squirrels!' Rose squealed.

'Sorry, Stevie. It's just that Rose woke me up and said that Shadow wasn't at the home, so we went looking for her. We found this white cat on the way back, and I let Rose keep it,' I gabbled.

'Well, keep both of the mangy beasts away from my office, do you hear me? If they cause any trouble, I will take it upon myself to take them both to the pound!' Eliza said this in such a stern voice that Rose and I knew not to argue.

We went back up to our room, and Rose put the new cat in the bathroom while I put Shadow outside the bathroom door. I opened the door a crack and let both cats see each other. Rose crawled out of the toilet and sat down on the edge of my bed, eager to see if the cats liked each other. We knew Shadow had taken a liking to her, but we had to make sure. We didn't want any accidents happening.

While most cats would have hissed and backed away, Shadow immediately jumped at the kitten.

'Shadow! No!' I shouted. But instead of biting and scratching the kitten, she just purred and groomed it with her tongue as a mother cat would do to her baby.

'Oh, does Shadow think the other kitty needs a bath?' said Rose.

'I'm not that sure, actually,' I mumbled.

We left the two cats to get used to each other while Rose and I went down to have supper. I ran into Brodie on the way down the stairs, and he stuck his tongue out at me and tried to trip Rose to get her to fall.

'Ouch!' cried Rose as she fell to her knees at the foot of the stairs. Brodie laughed and ran up the stairs two at a time.

'Are you okay, Rose?' I asked, bending down beside her.

'Yeah, my knees just hurt a bit,' said Rose, getting up and dusting herself off.

'Good. You didn't half give me a fright too! Let's hope that Eliza didn't hear that,' I said. Eliza would usually shout at the person who was hurt for being clumsy and not the person who inflicted the pain on said person. 'Remember to think about a name for your cat too.'

'I already know what I want to name her: Pearl! Pretty Pearl!' The mumbled those last two words over and over again all through dinner.

4

Gone

When we got back to our room, we found the two cats sleeping right in the middle of the bed. Rose giggled quietly and put her hand over her mouth to muffle her laughter.

'So … where are we going to sleep?' Rose whispered after a few moments.

'Dunno,' I mumbled.

'Will we have to wake up the kitties? I don't want to wake them up!' she said sadly.

'No, we won't wake them up. It would probably upset them,' I said, but after a few hours of playing about half of the two thousand board games that Stevie left in my closet, we were both exhausted. Our legs were asleep from sitting on the floor, and the cats had been playing with each other's tails.

We eventually had to carry the cats out of bed, but they slept soundly in our arms as we put them together in Shadow's bed.

A few months later I woke up to Shadow and Pearl licking my face and Rose gently pinching my arm.

'Star! Star! Stevie and Eliza want us!' she whispered.

'What is it now?' I mumbled sleepily.

'I hope it's not about the cats; I don't want to get rid of them,' Rose muttered.

We got dressed, went downstairs, and saw Stevie and Eliza talking to each other in the kitchen doorway.

I walked up to them and asked why they had called us so early in the morning.

'We've decided that you and Rose are both going to start going to school. You spend far too much time with those cats and are oblivious to everything else! It's absolutely ridiculous. You need to get out and socialize!' said Eliza sternly.

That was the one perk of staying at the home. No school. We could stay home all day, muck about, watch TV, and do all kinds of stuff we couldn't do at school. The best part was that everyone else had to go to school, so we had the whole home to ourselves. Stevie still hadn't found a place for us to go to school, so we just stayed home and went about our business. Hannah, the woman who looked after us while Eliza and Stevie were out running errands, was a heavy sleeper, so we could grab food from the fridge whenever we got a bit peckish.

Eliza woke us up from our happy memories by giving us both a hard poke in the back and telling us to stop daydreaming. 'Get dressed because you're going to school whether you want to or not.'

When we were back in our rooms, I suddenly realized something. Who would feed the cats? Pearl and Shadow meant the world to Rose and me, and we could never bear it if they were handled or treated wrongly. I couldn't leave food for them because Hannah was a scatterbrain; if she saw the food before the cats, she would probably throw it out. I pulled on my jeans and favourite T-shirt, which had a photo of a cat with a moustache and glasses on it; put on my Converse; and grabbed my backpack.

I went to the bathroom, where Rose was getting changed, and walked in. Rose was looking at herself in the mirror, nibbling her lip.

'Star? Who's going to look after our cats? I don't want them to starve!'

'Of course they won't starve! Don't be so stupid, Rose.' I was being mean to her simply because I was worried about it myself, but when I saw Rose's face crumple, I felt horrible.

'I'm so sorry, Rose,' I said, hugging her. 'Say something mean to me – go on.' Rose looked at her feet and mumbled something about my being upset with her.

'What? I'm not angry at you, you noodle. I'm just worried about the two cats,' I replied.

Just as I finished saying that, both the cats woke up and popped their heads out of the blanket that we had put on them to keep them warm. They both looked so comical that Rose and I started giggling uncontrollably at the sight of them. When we stopped laughing, we went downstairs and saw Stevie and Eliza whispering about something.

'Which school are we going to, Miss Eliza and Miss Stevie?' I asked, bobbing a curtsy to them.

'Oh, it's not just for the day. We've decided to send you to boarding school,' Eliza said hotly.

'What's boarding school?' asked Rose quietly.

'It's a lovely place where you can take lessons and learn. You will have a nice bedroom, much nicer than the one you have here,' said Eliza. It was as if she were trying her hardest to get rid of us.

'Y-you mean we'll l-live there?' Rose stuttered.

'Yes, but it's for your own good. You'll be much happier there. Besides, we already have way too many people crammed together in the home as it is. Children are going to have to start sleeping under the kitchen table soon!' Stevie boomed in that loud sing-song voice you usually only used for scared toddlers.

'So you send us off like blimmin' parcels to a place we've never even seen? And what about the cats? Who's going to look after Shadow and Pearl!' I replied. I had never been to a boarding school before, but I didn't think they allowed animals there, and I didn't want to take any chances.

'Those pesky varmints should be put to sleep! I'm taking them to the vet as soon as you two troublemakers leave,' Eliza muttered under her breath so she wouldn't scare Rose. But Rose had much better hearing than Eliza thought. Rose's lip wobbled, and she burst into tears a few seconds after Eliza finished her sentence.

'Eliza, see what you've done! You've reduced the poor mite to tears!' Stevie said sadly. 'Looks like you owe somebody an apology!'

'No! She deserves to know the truth. Those cats are corrupting their minds!'

'Whoa, whoa, whoa! They're just cats, Eliza! They're rather sweet things, if I do say so myself. They're not evil!' shouted Stevie, crouching beside Rose.

'I don't like Eliza anymore. She's mean,' mumbled Rose. Eliza looked appalled and then did something no normal person would do. She slapped Rose round the face. Rose turned red in the face, stamped on Eliza's foot, and charged up the stairs, past the large crowd that was huddled at the top. Brodie was there, and he stuck his tongue out at Rose. Rose sprayed him in the face with spit by blowing what was probably the biggest raspberry known to man. I found it hilarious, but Brodie probably didn't. Hey, anger makes us do crazy things! I once punched a fat man in the belly after he tried to push in front of me on a water slide! Sure enough, he went back to his place.

'Rose? Rose sweetie? Oh, please come down. We won't send you to boarding school!' Stevie called up the stairs. I think Rose was either being stubborn or she knew that Stevie wouldn't really let her take the matter into her own hands. Stevie eventually gave up and turned to Eliza, who was snorting like a bull.

'How dare you! Get out of this establishment right this instant. I cannot believe you could have done that to a seven- year-old!' shouted Stevie. She glanced over slightly and realized all the children that had huddled at the top of the stairs were still there. 'Go on – scram! Go back to your rooms!' she added in her sternest tone.

'Good. I hate this place anyway! I wanted to leave as soon as that girl arrived. I knew she was a troublemaker all along. I wouldn't be surprised if she was the spawn of the devil himself!' Eliza screamed, spraying spit everywhere. I badly wanted to scream 'Hey, say it; don't spray it!' right in her ear, but I had enough sense to stay silent. I hadn't yet processed that she was talking about me. It was only when Stevie looked at me worriedly, nibbling her lip, that I twigged that she thought *I* was the troublemaker. I stayed calm and bit my lip to stop myself, but I rushed up the stairs when I heard Rose shriek my name.

'Star! The cats! They're gone!' she screamed.

'What? What do you mean? They can't be gone. I'm sure I shut the door behind me!'

I found Rose weeping bitterly on the bed. Tears and snot were running down her face, which was purple in rage and sadness. Just then, as if on cue, Stevie rapped on the door with her knuckles as I was desperately trying and failing to calm down Rose. But if I'm honest, I was terrified too.

I knew that I would never be able to get over it if Shadow was hurt, and I was also concerned about Pearl for Rose's sake. I shouted at Stevie to leave us alone and looked around the room to try to calm down the crying seven-year-old.

'Have you checked the cupboards and closet?' I gabbled hastily.

'Yes! I've checked everywhere I can think of!

'Have you taken a peek in the toilet?' I said, trying to make her laugh. She took me seriously and scampered into our cramped bathroom. She trudged out and muttered, 'Nothing in there but our stuff.' I suddenly knew what I had to do. I needed to find those cats, and I was going to, no matter what. I didn't care if Stevie stopped Rose from coming along. I didn't care if the home exploded in a burst of fire. All I cared about at that moment was finding the cats.

5

The Inn

Okay, so *maybe* it was a terrible idea running away from the home with Rose without any idea where we were going, no money, and no sense of direction.

I should probably talk about how I ended up in a hospital with Rose beside me and the cats at either end of our beds.

We'd left the home with our backpacks, our favourite possessions, and enough food to feed a small herd of dirty llamas. We set off down the road at two in the morning to find the cats.

Rose groaned halfway through our trek, and we had to stop at the nearest place we could find.

We ended up in the burnt forest where I first found Shadow. Sure enough, we saw a trail of paw prints leading all the way out of town and into the mountains. We walked until it was dark, and then Rose spotted a little inn and suggested we go ask for a room. I agreed but said we had to do a runner in the morning due to the fact that we had no money.

We went inside and rang the bell for assistance. There were about three or four old men sitting on stools next to us, downing pints of beer. The stale smell of ale floating around the room was nauseating enough to make you sick!

We rang twice more. No answer. I became so frustrated that I thumped my fist on the table and shouted into the kitchen. A grimy-looking man in a vest came shuffling behind the desk, quietly mumbling, 'Don't get your knickers in a twist. What do you two rascals want?'

'We want the cheapest room you've got,' I said, trying hard not to let my voice break. The man stared at us wide-eyed.

'Where are your parents?' he asked, nudging his friends.

'Why do you want to know?' I muttered.

'Cheek! You think you can just waltz in here and ask for a room? Get out right now!' he shouted. I saw Rose's lip tremble and was prepared to argue back, but a kind-looking lady with long tied-up blonde hair came through.

'Give the poor dears a room, Lewis! They look tired and hungry!' She spoke with a thick Russian accent. She managed to look feminine even though she was in a bar with about twenty-five men, at least three of whom were vomiting. Rose smiled happily, although I didn't know why.

'Excuse me! You don't tell me what to do! You cook and serve us and nothing more! I could easily push you out along with these two girls here!' Lewis shouted.

Rose's face looked as if she wanted to slap Lewis. Hard. I put my hand on her shoulder to refrain her.

'Go ahead! You'll never find any other respectable woman to work here anyway! Heck, you'll never find anyone around here. We're right at the bottom of a mountain. The only people stupid enough to venture out here are drunk old men who don't know where they're going!' She glanced at us. 'Except for you two dears. You both look very bright to me.'

She motioned for us to come behind the bar and stand in the kitchen. I wasn't that sure about doing so, but it was our best bet, as I didn't fancy arguing with Lewis any longer and risk scaring Rose anymore. We stepped into the grimy kitchen and breathed out in relief and because of the smell.

'I know it isn't up to standards, but I keep it as clean as I can. This place used to be really ritzy and a posh five-star restaurant until Lewis came here. All sorts used to come here, you know, but no mad old men and stupid women. I'm Lizzie, by the way.'

Lizzie carried on while she led us up to our room. It was rather small, with a sloped roof and one tatty old bed, but it was better than nothing.

6

Leaving

"Th-thank you,' stuttered Rose as we ducked into the room. Lizzie smiled sweetly, and Rose smiled back weakly. Lizzie eventually let us unpack our things. I had my sketch pad, and Rose had her sock monkey named Boop-Boop. I kept my money in the drawer next to us. We went to lie down, squashed up on the single bed, and sighed deeply.

'Star?' asked Rose. 'Will we ever find the cats?' I had just put that thought out of my mind, and now it flew back in again.

'I hope so, Rose. I really do hope so.'

We fell asleep even though it was still light outside, and there was a commotion downstairs in the lounge.

The next morning, we woke up and freshened up in the incredibly smelly bathroom. Seriously, when did they last clean that thing? We then walked downstairs with dark rings under our eyes. Lizzie was the first to notice our grimy condition and gave us some burnt yet cold hash browns. They tasted like coal dipped in vomit to me, but Rose seemed okay with them. At least they filled us up. We went to pack our bags.

'Star?' said Rose, shivering in the cold mountain air. 'Where are we going to stay when we climb the mountain?'

As I looked out the window, I finally processed the fact that we were actually at the base of a mountain in the middle of November. Weird! I'd thought I was just having some creepy panic-induced dream. Then I realized that one of us could get seriously sick because we didn't have jackets. I wiped down my mud-covered jeans and squeezed Rose's shoulder.

'I don't know, Rose. I honestly don't know. I guess I thought some magical answer would just pop up like in cartoons!'

'How about we ask Tobie if we can borrow his sled and husky doggies? I saw him park the sled outside and bring the huskies in with him.'

'Who's Tobie?' I asked. I knew some of the men and women who lodged here liked Rose, but I had never seen anyone with a sled and dogs.

'Look outside! He's leaving! Quick – let's try to catch up to him. I don't think he's let the huskies off their leads and onto the sled.'

'Rose? Did you wake up in the middle of the night and go downstairs or something?' I asked more to myself even though I addressed Rose. Her look said it all, and I knew I had hit it on the dot. I sighed.

I pressed my nose up against the window and saw a man who looked like a cross between Santa Claus and a Neanderthal. He was desperately trying to untangle two wriggling and squirming pups as the other four jumped about and frolicked in the crystal-white frost.

The youngest puppy, who was brown with broad shoulders and a bandaged ear, even got his tongue stuck to a small patch of ice. I chased after Rose, my bag bumping against my leg uncomfortably at each long stride.

Lizzie rushed out and asked for about a quarter of the actual payment due. I thanked her and hurriedly pressed some money into her hand.

We caught up to Tobie just as he was tying the last dog to the sled. He looked up at Rose and smiled.

'Hello, Rosy Cheeks!' he chuckled.

'Hi, Tobie!' squealed Rose.

'Hello, sir,' I mumbled quietly. He glanced at me and said hello politely, but he only seemed interested in Rose.

'So … what brings you here this early, you two? It's only six!' he tried to sound stern, but he was happy to take us up the mountain.

'Oh, thank you!' I cried.

'Before we leave, why do you want to go?' he asked. Rose nibbled her lip nervously.

'Well … you see,' muttered Rose quietly, 'we lost our two cats, Shadow and Pearl, and they mean a lot to us.'

Tobie looked at us and nodded his head solemnly. 'I know how you two feel. My old pup, Sugar, got lost too. When I found her and brought her home, she had been gone so long that she forgot my brother who lived with me! But she still remembered me, and I'm sure your cats will remember you too.'

'Thank you,' I whispered softly. I didn't know a buff guy like him could be so gentle!

'So shall we set off?' he asked

'You betcha!' laughed Rose.

7

Bats

As we left the inn, I was fascinated by the scenery and the frost-covered trees. Instead of a whip, Tobie gently patted the dog that was nearest to him on the flank and whispered something in his fluffy grey ear. Like magic, all the dogs ran forward and charged their way through the steep, winding mountain path.

Halfway up the mountain, Rose nudged me while I looked out at the icy rivers and miniscule people. I squeezed her hand, excited by the sensation of being pulled by dogs and going up a mountain.

'Star,' she whispered, 'are we nearly there yet?'

'No, Rose.'

'Can we play a game?'

'What type of game?'

'I spy.'

'Halfway up a mountain?'

'Yes,' Rose replied.

After a while, I gave up and decided to play. Rose did a few easy ones: 'I spy with my little eye, something beginning with *s*! Can you guess? Hey, that rhymes!' But she then went on to some hard ones, like *c*, *m*, and a. *A* was *air*. That girl was ruthless!

Suddenly, Rose breathed in sharply and told Tobie to stop the sled.

'Why, sweetie? Is something bothering you in that carrot-coloured head of yours?'

'Don't call me that,' she snapped. I could hear her voice cracking, though. I think she missed the home. But she soon regained her calm attitude. She knew the cats were our main priority.

Oh no! I thought. What would Stevie say when we get back? She probably wouldn't tell Rose off as much because she was only seven, but she would go absolutely loco on me!

She might even hit me! I'd gotten enough of that from Brodie and his cronies (hey, another rhyme!), but I promised myself I would not cry. I would not let her see how scared I was. I would be *strong*!

Or I could just break down and cry so she would cuddle me, say sorry, and give me some of those tasty-looking biscuits that she kept on her desk.

Either that or she would totally ignore me and continue ranting on about how irresponsible I was and how disappointed she was in me.

As I was thinking about this, Rose was smoothly slinking out of the sled and into a dark and narrow cave. I snapped out of my daydream and glanced at Tobie anxiously. He nodded to signify that I should follow her.

'I'll join you in a second. There's a torch in the pack. Be careful and don't go in more than a couple of metres,' he said.

Wait, wait, wait … A pack? So there was food in there and stuff? I grabbed the torch and hurriedly trotted into the cave.

I flicked the torch on, and a beam of yellow light shone out, illuminating the cave.

'Great, now I can see just how narrow and enclosed the cave is!' I said.

I prowled around and saw Rose's flame-coloured hair crouched in a corner behind a rock. She was petting something. Something dark …

As I walked behind her, I felt something soft on my jeans. I looked down in a panic and saw two emerald-green eyes staring back at me.

'Sh-Shadow?' I stammered

'Pearl is here too!' said Rose, holding her cat up. Shadow meowed as if trying to say, *It's me! Don't look at her – focus on me!* I shone the light downwards and bent down, my legs shaking.

I clutched Shadow to my chest and staggered over to Rose. She was also locked in an embrace with Pearl, whose blue eyes were gleaming with happiness and relief, her face red with glee.

Well, that's what it looked like. Either that or she was suffering from oxygen loss by how hard Rose was squeezing her.

As we finished our cuddling session, we heard Tobie stumbling around and banging and tripping over the stalagmites that were protruding from the ground. Those are the long pointy thingies that that come up from the floor in caves.

'Rose? Star?' he called desperately, with a little more than anxiety in his voice. Hang on. How did he know my name? Oh well, he must have just heard Rose talking to me on the ride here.

'Rose? How did you know the cats were in the cave? You couldn't see more than a couple of feet in,' I said quietly.

'I-I don't really know. I just kind of sensed it,' she muttered.

8

Unusual

We explained everything to Tobie, and he agreed to take us back to the home and talk to Stevie about it. I also wanted to hear about how Eliza was doing; I still couldn't believe Stevie sent her packing like that! When I get there, her bed would become the official Pee-Pee Play Place for the cats.

We walked out of the gloomy cave with the cats trotting alongside us. We encountered a few angry spiders on the way, but the cats dealt with that. Also, I was starting to notice that Shadow's eyes were *glowing*. Weird!

We stopped off at the inn for some lunch. Lewis saw the cats and shrieked at us.

'How dare you bring such filthy vermin in my establishment? Get them out now or else there will be consequences!' he shrieked, yellowy-green spittle going everywhere. His face was red and puffy, and he was sweating as if he had just run a mile. Luckily, Lizzie came in to sort him out.

'Lewis. Lewis! *Lewis!* Calm down, you old windbag, and give them a chance. Julie would have wanted it, and you know it! Your sister had at least three dogs – so deal with the poor critters the same way you dealt with the dogs!'

Rose looked down at Pearl and ran up to the bedroom. I jogged after her, with Shadow perched like a parrot on my shoulder. When I arrived, Pearl was wearing a collar just like Shadow's, only with a yellow sun!

'Rose, where did you find that?' I asked quizzically.

'I found it in the cave. I was going to give it to Shadow, but then I remembered that she had her own collar, so I kept it for myself. Pearl had done a wee-wee right in the middle of the collar!' She giggled at the supposedly naughty word.

'Oh well, it's not as if anyone's going to find it out here. We may as well keep it.'

As I was saying these words, out of the corner of my eye, I saw the moon and the sun start to glow. A blinding flash of light appeared, and the two cats got pulled together. With a deafening meow, the two cats were absorbed into a blue gem-like ball.

After the light cleared, and Rose stopped shouting and crying out in pain that her eyes were too small for this ose, I saw the most amazing thing I had ever seen.

The two cats were absorbed into one! It now had a white face with a black moon around the left eye. The body was black and had strange tribal-looking white markings all over it, making the cat's fur contrast eerily with its eyes. The eyes were by far the strangest part. One was blue, and one was green, signifying that both cats had been welded into one. She was also frickin' giant!

'Wow …,' we both whispered, our jaws practically hanging open with awe.

'Meow.'

Then everything went black, and I had the sensation of rushing air all around me. When I opened my eyes and realized that I had fainted, I simply smiled to myself. I didn't know what happened, but I did know three things:

a) Something about the collars or the cats was magic. Not really sure which one.
b) We were never going back to the children's home.
c) These next few years were going to be a wild ride.

To my parents, Imane and Aziz; my
wonderful school, DESS; and to
all my teachers who contributed
to my education to let me do what
I have managed to achieve.

After their unexpected meeting at a
children's home in Sydney, Australia,
two girls, Rose and Star, find true
companions and make good friends
along the way. But after a while, the
two things that mean the most to
them go missing! Will they find their
feline friends before it's too late?

Printed in the USA
CPSIA information can be obtained
at www.ICGtesting.com
CBHW061803101024
15668CB00045B/728